Squirrel Monkeys

Written by Jo Windsor

In this book you will see squirrel monkeys.

You will see...

tails

jumping

babies

Squirrel monkeys are small monkeys. They have white faces and black noses.

Squirrel monkeys have lots of fur on their ears.

Squirrel monkeys call to other monkeys in the group. This keeps the group together.

But when there is danger, they will make a big, big noise. They will bark and scream.

Look out! Look out!

All the monkeys know there is danger!

Squirrel monkeys like to eat leaves, fruits, seeds, eggs, and insects.

When one monkey finds food, the others will come get it, too.

**Food, food!
Lots of food over here!**

Squirrel monkeys have hands with fingers and thumbs.

They hold on to the branches of the trees.

They have legs that are good for jumping from tree to tree.

They can go very fast.

A squirrel monkey has a long tail. The tail helps the monkey hold on to trees.

When it walks along a branch, it holds on to the branch with its tail. It will not fall off.

A squirrel monkey uses its tail to…

hold on to the tree	Yes? No?
get food	Yes? No?
fly	Yes? No?

A squirrel monkey has one baby at a time.

When a baby is born, it holds on to its mother's fur.

It drinks its mother's milk and sleeps in her fur.

The baby will ride around on the mother's back.

The baby holds on tight!

When the mother is jumping from tree to tree,
the baby will not fall off.

The baby holds on with its...

tail	Yes? No?
hands and feet	Yes? No?
teeth	Yes? No?

The monkeys in the group will help take care of the baby until it is six months old.

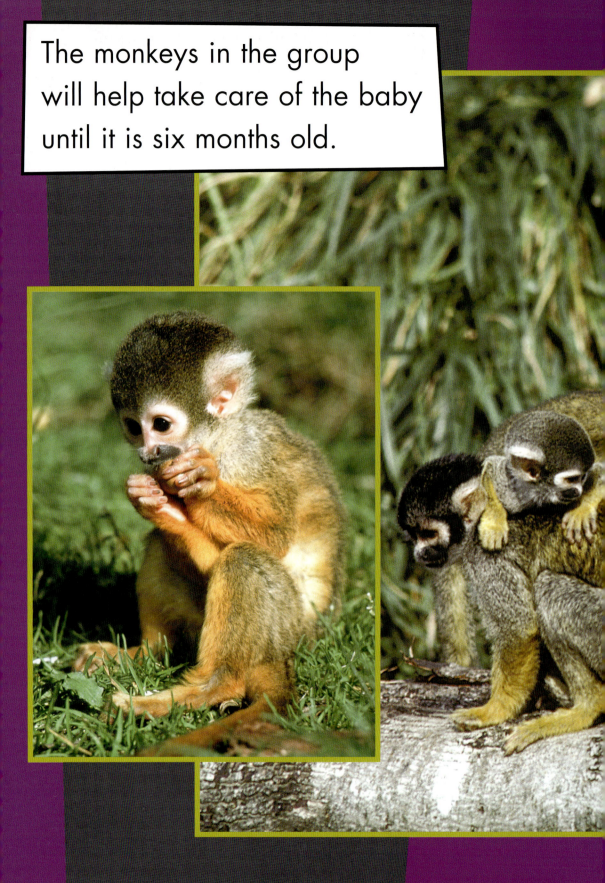

Index

babies . . 3, 16, 18, 20

danger 8

food 10

jumping 3, 13, 18

living
   in groups . . . 6, 8, 20

tails 3, 14

A yes/no chart

Squirrel monkeys can bark. **Yes? No?**

A squirrel monkey has a red nose. **Yes? No?**

Squirrel monkeys live in the water. **Yes? No?**

Squirrel monkeys eat insects and fruit. **Yes? No?**

Squirrel monkeys eat people. **Yes? No?**

Squirrel monkeys are good at jumping. **Yes? No?**

Word Bank

branch	fruit
ears	insects
eggs	seeds
face	thumb
fingers	